SLOW MIRACLE

To Cynthia and Carlos—
...friends in
poetry.

by

Christine
Swanberg

Christine Swanberg

Cover:
Elaine Hirschenberger, artist
Rich Hein, cover layout

Photo: Jeff Swanberg

Layout editor: Wayne Spelius

Editor: Carol Spelius

LAKE SHORE PUBLISHING
373 Ramsay Road
Deerfield, IL 60015

ISBN # 0-941363-11-2

price $9.95

DEDICATION

For Mark Rinaldi, my brother.

Because he could not, I do.

For all the gift bearers, teachers, and dreamers, who know that miracles are gradual and continuous, sometimes happening when we least expect them.

"Now there are varieties of gifts, but the same Spirit; and there are varieties of service, but the same Lord; and there are varieties of working, but it is the same God who inspires them all in everyone. To each is given the common manifestation of the Spirit for the common good."

. . . CORINTHIANS 12:4-7

"The miracles of the church seem to me to rest not so much upon faces or voices or healing power coming suddenly near to us from afar, but upon our perceptions being made finer, so that for a moment our eyes can see and our ears can hear what is there about us always."

. . . Willa Cather

FOREWORD

Christine Swanberg knows what she is doing. Exactly. She knows where she started and where she is going. She is writing poetry which proves it. In her first book, the poem "Ruminations on a Perfect May Day," suggests the early frustrations of the artist who would like to leave behind compromise and practicality for the hazardous pursuit of writing. The spirit of the artist, the creative gypsy, or "something" must be released. "Something wants out. / Something wants in . . . Exorcism is in order." This artist is seeking a way to let the gypsy roam, to express herself, to create her art.

Christine successfully plays all her roles: teacher, organizer, critic, community conscience, writer. But at an early stage in her career she determined her priorities and has been brave enough to work at becoming the poet she wants to be. Her four books of poetry to date prove her dedication is justified.

SLOW MIRACLE deals with art as obsession, as fun, and as religion. It includes clairvoyant insights into human character and global politics. It considers the personal, the philosophical, and the profound.

Perhaps the most surprising is the poetry which deals with soul and spirit. In the earlier books, acknowledgment and respect for the author's cultural and religious heritage are voiced, but in SLOW MIRACLE there is a personal, one-to-one, poet-to-creator rejoicing in the arrival at soul's maturity. The slow miracle seems to be the poet's own development -- slow because all worthwhile things take time --, miracle because a poet's self-revelation is always a miracle.

Christine Swanberg is a poet who has accepted the responsibility of her gifts, her intellect, her experience, her *giest.* The reader will be enlightened by SLOW MIRACLE and eager for whatever follows.

. . . *Rachael Burchard*

Rachael C. Burchard is critic, poet, and playwright. Books include JOHN UPDIKE: YEA SAYINGS (Southern Illinois University Press) and GREEN FIGS AND TENDER GRAPES (Wyndham Hall Press.)

To the Reader:

Writing poetry is an act of discovery; I don't know when I begin a poem where it will lead or what form it will take. These are surprises that happen as the poem takes on its own life -- sometimes meandering like a creek, sometimes gushing like a waterfall. To share this experience is both a privilege and a risk. To have a publisher such as Carol Spelius like the work enough to publish it is a privilege for which I am heartily grateful. To have an audience of readers is an honor. The risk, of course, is whether they will enjoy it.

I'd like to think that SLOW MIRACLE is the most accessible collection that I have written. Many of these have returned to the recognizable forms of sonnet, haiku, and dramatic monologue, partly because I wanted to discover how these traditional forms can shape a poem and partly because I find the process rewarding. The title, SLOW MIRACLE, cropped up in my journal a few times before I realized what it was meant to be. To a large extent, that title was the guiding force behind many of these poems, often leading to unexpected spiritual and artistic discoveries, which I hope readers will share.

. . . Christine Swanberg

Table of Contents

RETREAT

I was seeking guidance,
expecting the revelation of my life
to come searing like a brand,
a *C* for Christ, my namesake.
Missionary? Prophet? Wise Counselor?
Whose cross would I bear in my following?
What part of me would have to die?

Then came a still, small voice,
a Lady in Blue, her only yoke
a ribbon around her empire-waisted frock,
her face as calm as alabaster --
my own face greeting age with wisdom.
She carried a message in her plump hand:
"Live more spontaneously."

That night I dreamed she held a wand,
bright pink neon, incandescing,
and when she placed it in my hand,
it burned.

AFTER ADMIRING PEÑA'S PAINTING

Navidad de Santa Fe

In Peña's landscape, color glides as free
As midday sun or horses on the run.
Shadows leap like pimas from adobe.
Pueblos huddle like tribes under gun.
Three wise Indians bear gifts of the earth.
Sun-baked angel faces sculpted the same,
Serene, for they have found the place of birth
Of the Awaited, in whose eyes they claim
The glory of their meekness. Communion
Of earth, wind, fire, and stars. 0 Great Spirit
That lights the kiva and burns the piñon.
O sacred incense and loom of fire!
O Sangre de Cristo, the mountains call.
Feliz Navidad . . . Sisters, brothers, all!

THE DAY AFTER CHRISTMAS

Today I celebrate glorious nothing,
put my phone on cruise control
so no one can intrude upon my uncelebration.

Today is my true Sabbath,
a day when I am free to unplug
work, family, shopping, feast.

This day once was the blue pine
of too much everything too sweet
and stale, a tally of cookies,

relatives who say all the wrong things,
a day for crying over what has never been
and what will never be. But today

I claim nothing
but this good cup of coffee,
streak of blue in the skylight,

a frost terrarium of ferns,
conifers and feathers,
this old pen and used paper,

my good old ass
anchored in this chair, and just
hang out in this slow miracle.

WALKING ALONG THE ROCK RIVER

There were times
when walking here would not have been
enough, times my restless spirit
needed an ocean, not this river, serene
and simple. But today I thank each wild place
in this trip composite,
compassion winding like this river.
Let them be milk pods in a Hopi basket
woven serpentine, one spirit strand
placed wrong to prove we're human.

Just today, I hear
ice like windchimes,
wonder
how long they've sung their thousand
haiku, how long the sun has carved
these transient diamonds,
how the mallard's emerald chevron
came to be some vagrant stamp of evolution
holding a code I may never know --
this feather, fallen in the snow.

HAIKU PRELUDE

Crow in autumn --
look how the prisms shine
between his feathers.

* * *

November twilight --
in the icy blue sky
only crows cawing.

* * *

First morning snowfall --
on a neighbor's mountain ash
red, frosted berries.

* * *

First snow --
half eaten pears on bare branches
. . . and grackles.

* * *

Winter morning walk --
my plump, red hooded jacket
and cardinal watching.

ICE

"*But if I had to perish twice,*
I think I know enough of ice..."
--Robert Frost

A thick, deep patch of ice
beneath a scratch of snow,
a crazy slip, sound of ice cracking,
bone splitting into ice chips,
my leg breaks and my veins freeze.
I'm stuck to the driveway
like an ice cube in a tray,
hands clenched so tight
they carve icy half-moons
straight through my gloves.
I'm immobile as a block of ice,
feel like the wicked witch of the west,
want to scream, "I'm melting,"
fear I may turn into a puddle of myself.
Pain, dry ice searing from the inside out,
pain, like nothing I have ever known.
I no longer own my toes.

A nurse rubs a clove of ice
against my vein until it pops
into a small hailstone, injects
a toothpick made of ice, fills
my veins with freezing fog.
My leg is cast in a glacier,
propped on cumulous clouds,
covered with a bag of ice.
In the dark, the nurses, snow angels,
feel my feet, their fingers

like snowflakes land and melt
throughout the night. My morphine
machine drips like a stalactite,
a numbing mercy in this cave,
where my eyes fill with sleet
when morning brings an icicle
at my window.

PERFECT HEALING

I thank the steel
that reinforced my bones
like armour,
the surgeon, scalpel, scar
for their stories
of courage, mending, trust,
the crutches
for making me hate them,
the muscles
for coming out of cocoons --
slow miracles
I almost didn't believe --
but especially I thank
the bones
for spinning calcium webs
stronger
because they were broken.

AT THE BOOKSTORE

A large, apple-faced man
who will look like Santa soon
pushes me against the counter
and gruffly asks if the books
on agoraphobia are in yet.
The owner goes in search of them
while the big guy bellows on:
Wife's been agoraphobic ten years.
Only leaves the house to see
the chiropracter. Joined
an agoraphobia support group.

Sighing, I set down my May Sarton
JOURNAL OF A SOLITUDE and my
Ferlinghetti ENDLESS LIFE,
cannot help myself and blurt:
Trouble is, no one shows up. Right?

He doesn't get it. Keeps blabbing.
Suddenly I think of Lot's wife,
want to turn into a pillar of salt
and make the fat man lick me.

The owner checks him out first,
which takes a lot of time,
then says: Why Chris, I didn't know
you had a mean streak.

As I write my check for $13.68,
I am beginning to understand
the old goat's wife.

LOT'S WIFE

It wasn't that there were so many friends
Or that my life there had been so perfect.
It's just that how you look at it depends
On whose scheme of things you hold in suspect.
What was it to me that men were lovers
Or that a goat or two were glorified?
I never cared how others spent their hours.
I kept a good house and was occupied
In covenanted duties. It was a life.
It was all I knew. And what would you do
If someone said, "Don't look back"? Like a knife,
The words hit their mark. Mind bleeding, I knew
My fate. I had to be the one to look
And turn to salt. A lesson in their book.

IN EPHESUS

That's too
bad, the young
Turk said
when I told
him my name
was Christine.
I do not like
your God, he
answered when
I asked why.
It's a good
thing my name's
not Ruth, I
said as the
blood-red sun
splashed the
pillars yellow.

SHEPHERDESS OF SAMOS

I have no father to mumble worry-beads,
no mother to tell me the ways of women,
only this old woman and these goats.

Each day I go to the Temple of Hera
to pray for a man and a house of my own.
I say: "Bless Ephthansia, for she is good.

Every day we make bread,
and she gives me wine, but
do not let me die a servant to her."

The men have gone to Ephesus.
They are tired of fishing,
and the women here are dull.

Perhaps they will bring me an ankle bracelet
such as the maidens of Artemis wear
before they lure men into the temples.

This island is greener than all others.
The figs, olives, and grapes grow larger,
and nowhere does this purple vine

ring such fragrance. On the ledge
of this mountain I will wait
as my staff makes a shadow on my ankle.

I will unbraid my hair, fill it
with moonlight, the fragrance of vines,
and the salt of the sea wind.

Soon I must jangle these bells
and gather the goats into the valley.
In the distance, you can see them returning.

See the moon shine on lifted winesacks
in their shaft of cedar, spraying sea
on the moon's path that connects the islands?

Tonight we will dance, arms clasped
in slow circles, then faster circles,
until we can no longer trace the moon.

MOON SONNET

O Moon! You rule stronger than a mother.
Egg-shaped, hooded captor of cycle and tides!
You move through us, surprising as ether,
And in your dust filled, cratered heart resides
The secrets of the universe. Turn. Turn.
Shadowed globe whose pull we cannot escape.
Let us flow again with you and relearn
The secrets lost in the alchemist's cape.
Though we have turned ourselves from you
Like lovers lost or married for too long,
We return by night to your wheated hue
Wherein our tempests quell in moonsong.
We could not leave you even if we tried.
In our own secret centers you abide.

AFTER A PERFORMANCE OF *LUTHER*

You were everyone who has ever known
Torment of the soul that questions always,
Who knows the spirit like the wind full-blown
Will rock your branches and leave its mysteries
To faith alone. You sought and found a chasm.
Like Jesus in the marketplace, you whipped
Fetters from the church and began the schism
To free the world from dogma that had gripped
Its peasant heart. The bliss of ignorance
Was not enough for you. To merely glance
Upon the word would not reveal its fruit.
To know the tree of life, become its root,
Which like a narrow path is hard and steep.
To know the Shepherd is to be his sheep.

IN THE LAND OF MILK AND HONEY

In the land of milk and honey,
we were given all the gifts of the earth,
freely as an eagle soaring over mountains,
freely as a cactus flower in bloom.
Our lands sparkled like emerald crystals.
In our orchards. global fruit hung like lanterns,
lanterns that might have lit the world,
lanterns that might have fed the world.
We had the keys to the kingdom
but our tumid soil crumbled through our fingers
as our irrigation flowed freely as the Nile.
Even our arid deserts yielded fruit.
For we were the land of genesis.
To us nothing was denied.
Not water, soil, nor fire.

We were given the gifts of numbers and chemicals.
What the other people of the world called magic,
we called technology, and we ate it daily.
It was the bread of life; we were one with it.
It became the very language that we spoke.
It became the air we choked on.
And so our prophets wanted profits.
"*What profits a man to gain the world*
and lose his soul?"
We prayed to one god and served another.
Our minds became calculators.
Our eyes sparkled with dollar signs.
Our poets had no audiences.
And our leaders spoke in parables,
their tongues walled by invisible shields.
"*Our capacity to destroy*

will keep us from destruction."

In the land of milk and honey,
we could build anything.
Great edifices touched the skies like monoliths.
Great flying machines soared over our houses,
which became empty palaces but were a marvel
to the world that always watched us,
revered us, feared us, for we touched everyone.
Whatever we had, everyone wanted.
Whatever we did, everyone wanted to do.
And it came to pass that the big crystals were stolen,
and everyone knew the secret of the atom.

We were the world's greatest help
for we possessed the gift of healing,
but the world wanted what we had,
and we gave them war machines
until everyone was equal but no one was healed,
and the diseases we had the power to cure
still ravaged us like the earthquakes
we could predict but could not stop,
for we knew about the faults
that ran along the ocean floor
and stopped in our most fertile valleys
for they rumbled and roared and swayed beneath us
as the chasm grew wider.

We knew about the other faults too,
the ones that sat in our souls like great ravens,
the ones that obscured our purpose.
We ignored and chose the darker journey,
chose to dangle the keys to the kingdom,

the skeleton keys that might have opened paradise
but flipped the lid of Pandora's box
and left us open to destruction.

In the land of milk and honey,
we jangled the keys to the stars themselves.
We hunted stars as if they were great mammoths,
as if we might own even them.
We knew the secret of the crystals,
the invisible secrets of the molecules, which we
smashed into great puffing volcanoes of cement that
stored its poisonous lava in the earth's bowels.
The crystals might have exploded into hope for all,
but in our deserts, the eyes of lizards turned red,
the eagles lost their will to live, hiding
from the crystals that bled and split the air.
And as the gifts of air and fire fused,
the keys to the kingdom fell into the chasm.

And our leaders spoke in parables.

BLINDED BY THE LIGHT

You spent fifteen years writing it all down
as if the first time wasn't enough.
From the shanty houses of old Da Nang
to the jungle trenches where you laid mines
and watched your buddies get blown away
with shrapnel, DNT, weed and LSD.
You kept the stats intact in your clean mind:
One in five will never see home again.
One in three will not see their bodies whole.

Nam is a strange place to get religion.
Like Saul, you entered a persecutor.
You thought you knew the enemy but found
dominoes don't hold against the knowledge
that you live among friends who rape children,
rob graves, and plan to shoot your captain soon.
How could you eat anything when you knew
the man beside you set a rocket up
a girl -- she was a spy -- then let it fly?

They did not tell you one in two goes mad.
When you entered that cave, how could you
know whether your mother really called you?
How could you know it wasn't God who called,
saying, *Live, Captain. Live. It is worth it.*
And, my friend, whose book I read, you must know
that the road from Damascus still burns,
and the sand will singe your eyes like napalm,
and your poisoned skin will fall off like a snake's,
and when the scales drop off, you will see it
coiled, only whiteness blinding you now.

OPPENHEIMER

I cannot get beyond the face in the photo.
Are the large, languid eyes blue
like a clear desert sky?
Are they the pale amber of grain?
Or have they burned
Into the color of dust?
There is a wide gap between the brows,
a space large enough for a third eye.
The eyes do not seem mad,
or brilliant,
but if I look close enough,
is that the radiance of a thousand tears?
The eyes are human enough,
but the rest of the face is lean
and polished, waxy and pale.
There is little flesh.
Does this man even like food,
or does he live on thought
or particles of air
like those in a secret Indian sect?

The ears are small and pointed like an otter's.
There is no flesh on the lobe.
The cheekbones are low and delicate.
The lips are small and still.
He is lighting a curved black pipe --
a prized possession?
The match burns into a small trinity,
lit by his huge incongruous hands,

hands, mottled like trout,
that have a life outside the mind,
hands that light the furnace of the world.

The chin and the forehead are regular.
They are not strong.
There is nothing wrong in the face.
No hint of deformity.
No extra skin
though the Adam's apple is sharp
and the neck seems red and radiated.
The thin white hair is closely cropped.
The entire body seems to lean forward
as if there was a large hand on the shoulder.

When I look into this photo
I do not feel anything.
It is as if I am looking
into an aquarium. What is inside
comes from another world
from a depth I do not recognize.
But what I really want to know, Robert,
is how you felt
when your friend, Kenneth Bainbridge, said,
"Now we are all sons of bitches."

WHERE I TEND MY HORSE

Sometimes at farms nearby
a horse turns up missing --
the work of rustlers
who lure the gentlest,
the ones who'll take sugar
from moonlit palms,
follow up the ramp,
then to a slaughterhouse
across state lines.

I've dreamed of my horse often
these last fifteen years.
Last night she stood on the stairs
to my attic, balanced
and graceful as a ballerina.
Again I sensed she was sad,
missing me, though I know
this is projection. So today
I'll spend time brushing out
her winter coat, let her hair fly
like dandelion fluff
in the old barn.
We'll go way out,
canter Johnson's cornfield
to the Wicket River,
where an egret startled me last week.

Bright white, lost,
its fragile legs seared
by the icy current.

The Dreamer's Dictionary says
the horse once symbolized the sun
but later lust to Christians.
For Shamans, the horse meant sacrifice.
Today I thought I saw the egret again
but it was only a feed bag flapping,
caught in a stump, and I remembered
how one spring I found a boot
wedged in the May apples
and white panties crumpled
like a dish rag, glaring
from a patch of trillium.

DARK NIGHT OF THE SOUL

It may come in a trench like shrapnel,
burning like a bullet,
fire-seed that never leaves the body,
knowledge you refuse to own
until all walls of denial fall
and you stare into the blackest city
like Lot and know you can never turn back.
Or it may come when no pieces
of the puzzle called your life fit,
despite your best intentions,
and reason shrivels like a rotten apple.

First it feels like poison.
Then you feel the snake inside you.
My friend, I tell you there are choices
in this powerlessness, I swear,
if only you do not feed the snake.
I say: Give it nothing. No bread.
No words. No medicine or money.
Speak with no one who finds the snake
fascinating. Pay no one to charm it.
Beware of anyone who says it can be tamed.
To starve the snake, you must wait

and feel it eat you, but trust:
the snake will suck its own poison
and die. Then you will know the truth,
and the truth shall set you free.

TAPE

Friday, February 13,
and a bright pink Valentine arrives,
taped twice,
meaning it's from Aunt Libby.
She'd wrapped
a Band-Aid around the finger
a wasp had stung, knowing
it was the ritual I wanted,
the All better now.
Circled in white tape,
electrodes strung around my brother's crown,
like those gummed reinforcements
that keep paper from ripping from binders,
or the tube straight
into my mother-in-law's heart,
its walls dripping,
its floor filling with water
like a limestone basement
with no sump pump in spring.
Those
whose parting tears a little
then leaves the scars we tend like roses
when we finally reach the age
when all the bad news sticks,
the past glues us in,
and we can never be too careful.

BURN OUT

At first it's the virus
you can't seem to shake,
three small screws
boring into your neck,
a frown in your rearview mirror.
Then you catch yourself
sighing at lunch, wondering
why you spend so much time
with people you don't love.
You think you're going deaf
or everyone is mumbling.
You dream of soiled clothes
and wake to find them hanging
in your closet like skeleton keys.
Though you want to sleep forever
you wake earlier each day
until the night is a black dwarf
hiding in the corner
and even your old friend coffee
turns against you. You forget
your lipstick, then your name.

AN ENGLISH TEACHER'S SONNET

Give me consonants snapping like snare drums,
the difference between a *T* and a *D*.
Serve me a whole slice of bread, not just crumbs.
A tangerine's not a dromedary.
Speak vowels tunnel-shaped or sharp as skateblades.
Send me sentences that flow from the top
of the mountain, then roar over cascades.
Let them shout clear and frothy 'til they stop
for commas, rocks and pebbles that protect
the stream from gushing. Please, say what you mean.
Words, like water, can become polluted too.
Think of language, a gift crisp and clear.
Long for great, live words to reel in like fish.
Fry them up, digest them, and be nourished.

FOR DEE GREENE

1917-1984

You sang opera at the Met
made it big in Hollywood
trapsed across the cover of TIME
with the Three Stooges
like Dorothy in the Wizard of Oz
but you called it right
when you said,
"If I give up teaching,
I give up my life's blood,"
even though you were shuffled
from school to school
until at sixty-six, you ended
in this room with its decrepit boards
with "Green sucks" scrawled in the corner.

You wouldn't talk about your diamonds
or the medicine you took between classes,
why you weren't in a California home
for old actresses,
why you returned
to this cruel Illinois winter
and your mother's house, lilacs
pressing against the kitchen window
like weary ghosts,
how you came to be so large
that every stair was a hurdle.

Dee, was it unrequited love?
Were the reruns just reminders
of risiduals never paid,
or had you enough of stages?
No. You would not be old
with those ochre eyebrows
question marks that read,
"Is this all there is?"
You would not be that old comedienne
with dyed Lucille Ball hair
green eyeshadow crimping
in your bloated eyelids. No.
You would never be
that great iguana of the nursing home.

FOR LEO RINALDO

Your other teachers think I'm crazy
for thinking it's your dignity
that keeps you from smiling
for thinking it's the fear
you haven't named that flashes
in your eyes, sullen
with the latest drug
they say you're dealing.

Your records show a bright child
six addresses
three stepfathers
and no address for your real one
whose name you still hold.
Once you lived with your grandmother
who must have been the one
who taught you that incongruous
thank you
the only formal courtesy you own
that shaky stamp of civility
about to peel off soon.

Still, you're clean
and your demeanor's self-possessed
and regal as a cat's
but ready to pounce
capable of a quick kill
without expression
perhaps without remorse.

Baby, you're jailbait
if someone doesn't get to you
before you make the big score
and your fine name
reads like a mobster's
and your other teachers say,
"He never smiled
but he was clean
and always said thank you,"
if someone doesn't get to you
and let you know
all of us are puzzles
with missing pieces, irretrievable
as letters never written.
The trick is not to fall
through the holes.

FOR CLARA, THIRD HOUR

I picked up all your hints:
white Goya hands,
white enameled Merlin nails,
funky, soft-textured clothes,

fuzzy striped socks,
ironic suede bowling shoes,
and the glasses robbed
from John Lennon's grave.

Phantom incarnation born too late!
You don't belong to the Atari Age,
digging Zelda, Zen, the Dylans,
and owning the limited "White" album.

What antenna guided you to Hamlet
and Heathcliff? I see you
wrapped in an old afghan,
Lady MacBeth cat in your lap,

late into the night
reading, reading, reading.

A STUDENT CONTEMPLATES A PICKLED BRAIN

Looking out the laboratory window
into a Midwest sky so blue
it seems this summer lushness
pulls it closer,
it's hard to think this great
anemone in a sea of formaldehyde,
this grand gray cauliflower,
enormous sponge filled with magic
and miracles, this quieted Medusa,
coventry of worms,
cavernous fossil,
this labyrinth of impulse
with lights as plentiful as the stars
which even now incandesce unseen,
is a mere computer matrix,
or a ball of clay molded on its own
with centers that control,
for example, how I want to now
bask in the incomprehensible sun,
let beads form between my breasts,
let you lick them into an ectasy
no science can explain.

CAMILLE

Flipping off the switch
of our Friday night foreign video
about another would-be artist
whose temperament drives her mad,
this time Camille,
Rodin's inspiration, lover,
apprentice, confined
her last thirty years
to a mental institution,
I think of the want-it-so-bad poets
I've known these past few years:
the young who wonder why no one
pays good money for their anger,
the old who bore us with sentiment
and genealogy,
the scholars whose tight-lipped ramblings
etch a place for them in grants,
the women writing ugliness to prove
they are not victims,
the confessors who write compellingly
how they cannot touch a dying parent,
the manic who dream they're writing epics
before mastering the line,
the poetry group status climbers,
the religious for trivializing the spirit
with children's rhymes,

the gay who feel they must teach us
the error of our moderation,
the genital writers masturbating
at the podium,
the performers for creating yet another
bastard art form only a drunk could love,
those too pure to risk rejection,
but especially I think of you
because you're so damn good
you don't need me to tell you so.

Remember: Poetry is not a board game
like Monopoly. You pass Go on your own
with or without $200. My friend,
there's no Boardwalk unless you imagine it.
There is no win or lose.
Poets are not gods.
There is no muse but you.

AFTER WATCHING *VINCENT AND THEO* AT THE FINE ARTS CINEMA

At first it is obsession:
Van Gogh painting as no one else,
painting until he is the seed in *Sunflowers,*
the star in *Starry Night,*
swabbing the deck of his palette
with child fingers, licking
cobalt blue, primary yellow,
bringing them to his lips
until color sticks to the roof of his mouth
like a communion wafer,
dabbing and drying, his tongue parched
like Christ's touching vinegar.

"Art is not religion," he's warned.
But to be an artist means to break
all rules, or does it?
Do we demand such chronologies of madness
finally tiring of ourselves
rediscovering how little the hidden reveals
about the unknown, no matter
how compelling the color or technique?

At last he thinks he's God.
"We are all God," he says, self-portrait
after self-portrait, paint
like crusty worms, inching
into resurrection at Sotheby's,
ascension into the Big Money.

FOR KEITH JARRETT, AFTER A CONCERT

You're a teakwood puppet
with liquid fingers
staccato elbows strung
up to the god of jazz.
When she lifts her thumbs
you play each pebble in purple
streams, blue tumbling barrels
the white crashes of Niagara.
When she sends lightning
you're a charged kite, fingers
on fire, hair on end
flames fly in yellow light.

You lift off the stool
elbows high and frantic
like a praying mantis in leafy
smoke, and the god must have you
for her own, she pulls your spine
into her fists while your back arches
like a bow. Let the arrows sing their mark!
When subterranean lights turn red
the god of jazz lies at your feet.
You slip back slack and spent as a lover
in a cool pool of green applause.

BE-ATTITUDES

BEWARE:

the joker
for he hides a terrible secret

the woman who speaks too softly
for she carries a big stick

the woman who lives in her mother's house
for she wants to mother you

the rich mother-in-law
for she wants a clone

the wife who brags about her husband;
soon they will divorce

the husband who joins his wife on ladies' night;
he is having an affair

the mother who brags about her children;
she wants her freedom

the woman who brags about her freedom;
she wants a child

the workaholics
who will demean your need for pleasure

people who don't like cats
for they will never understand your independence

people who don't like dogs
for they cannot be bothered with affection

especially people from perfect families;
they understand close to nothing.

THE BUTTER GURU

Ananda of the shaven head
Ananda, the hitch-hiker
    we picked up in Gatlinburg
Ananda who drank tea with butter
Ananda who left golden pearls floating
    like water lilies on Lipton
Ananda of the greasy Rorschach
    left in every cup
Ananda, snatching sixteen pats of butter
    from a truck stop in the Smokies
Ananda, starting to scare us
Ananda, who ate our pizza and complained
    it wasn't vegetarian
Ananda who wouldn't leave us
    and might have been a convict
Ananda with my ten dollar bill
    buying groceries
    while we high-tailed out of town.

DREAM DURING THE PERSIAN GULF CRISIS

I am ice-skating on a pond
in January's white night.
My black skates carve a circle
like a huge communion wafer
as I spin faster and faster
like an oil drill. The ice cracks
and I ride my ice wafer down,
surprised that I am not cold.
Something warm, heavy, slippery, engulfs me.
When it reaches my eyes,
I am a cormorant sinking
into a slick, past placid stingrays,
a helmet, benign as a jelly fish.
I feel the tentacles of a man-o-war,
watch the white anenome's last dance,
until the merciful sand finally
wraps her hands around me.

MUSHROOMS

The day after I dreamed
the voice of God said,
"Your fears are mushrooms,"
I nibbled an omelet,
each brown stem a dare,
then stumbled into a poem
on how a pig ruts for truffles.
I saw chocolate toadstools
on sale at Crate and Barrel
and wondered who'd want them.
Later I watched a documentary
on poor, old Malcolm Lowry,
teased, the narrator said,
for his tiny penis. Flash
of white mushroom withering
behind a zipper.

In the evening I tell a friend
about the dream, but she
gets all political and serious.
"Don't you see it's the bomb
you're afraid of?"
I turn troll and tease,
"It's the Morel Majority's
got me down," then mumble
something about my fears
as harmless little fungi.

She says I’m into denial,
but last night a raspy voice
from the forest’s lush floor
croaked, "Freud is dead."
I woke, spores of laughter
erupting like puffballs.

IF DREAMS WROTE THE STORY

the killer poet would drive a black '37 Ford
like a fiend down Michigan Avenue, rutting
up alleys, past blue cats that shimmer
in window sills, backing right into
her puffy-faced stepfather.

Then the car would disappear, and they'd run
on a ledge until she turns to him, grabs
his throat, and finally, finally,
pushes him over for keeps.

Green pills would ooze from her mouth
until she spits them out and leaps
for joy, balancing like a tight-
rope walker while beneath her
the ledge becomes an ice

escalator. Then she would know
that to ride it down,
all she needs to do
is stand still.

DREAM #167035

I am in a locker room
colorless as a subway.
The odor of gasoline
is coming from a locker
when I realize I'm a clothes thief,
a glutton for soiled clothes.
No fetish -- I just want them,
the used sweated out remnants
of someone else's workout.
I lift the latch and surprise!
They fall out like an avalanche:
thirty pairs of pajamas,
balled up, stale as old lunches.
I cannot contain my joy.
I hadn't bargained for this:
purple stripes and polka dots,
some with tiny pink sailboats,
boxer waistbands, little snaps.
Wait. This dream doesn't make sense,
I say. Too late. I'm stuck with it.
The kindly union master wants to know
how I could stoop to such a thing.

TOTALLED

Bam! Someone's shooting tires.
It's the car. Bam! What the
hell swerving god grip the
Bam! I've lost control oh shit.
Duck! I'm rolling oh fuck!
Hold on to what? Corngravelditch
dashboard I must be rubberburning
dead but having odd noseatbelt
thought: "Eject before the flames!"
My legs are where? I feel nothing
must be ohohdead but amnot amnot.
Get out! No pain must be dead
should hurt but this can't be
heaven: WLS is playing
Cracklin' Neil Diamond's
I'm a rose upsidedown in glass
I smell the earth. Siren?
No. Tires whirring this is it
it's over don't panic your hand
is working see it feel the ground
around the window for glass?
O.K. O.K. Get out the window
watch it watch it. That's it.
You're standing in a cemetery
of cornlings? Oh God,
the car's an accordion. Shit.
I'll get a ticket. Whose
farm is this? Jesus, I'm alive
and standing. Not a scratch.
Not a fucking scratch. Oh
Jesus, Jesus, Jesus.

OLD FRIEND

Like the old winter tomcat
gone for months,
you have returned.

Here. Lap the warm milk of laughter
from this bowl of affection.
Chew morsels of understanding.

I will pull out burrs of disappointment,
brush away the bristles of loneliness,
cleanse your icy wounds from indifference.

Curl up on this loyal lap
and purr words of friendship.
No one takes your place at this hearth,

and the pantry is always stocked.

HAIKU INTERLUDE

Watching the sunset
from my old hammock --
flight of nighthawks.

* * *

Sunset mountain top --
orange stillness broken only
by swallows darting.

* * *

The horse and I
in the pine tree's shade --
a phoebe calling.

* * *

Beneath the pine trees
thousands of scented needles --
the horse's rustling.

* * *

Soon to be baskets --
rosehips and mulleins drying
along the roadside.

* * *

After the picking --
fragrance of concords
on blue fingertips.

* * *

Rose-breasted grosbeak
on the tip of a birch limb --
and blue sky.

COALTOWN SUMMERS

Mark, Illinois. Coal town.
One square mile of taverns,
bocci courts, a fire engine,
and three big coal dumps --
red clay, shale sphynx paws.
Across the tracks that dipped
into the edge of town,
a smaller berg slept:
Monkey's Nest, where the gypsies
and Polacks lived. They say
the gypsies came to town in summer
to sing and dance with a squeeze-box
for pennies and beers in the bars.

This pear tree, overgrown now,
still spawns these strange baubles,
so small, speckly, jasmine-moist.
Come late August, you couldn't
ride a bike or walk barefoot
in this alley. Pear puddles
and apricot grenades whipped
to pudding for a million honeybees.
This old grey wooden birdhouse here?
Grandpa's. He tamed finches
and rode his bike to the mine,
that one in the distance
with the crucifix careening on it.
Sat on his porch til the black lung
got him. Grandma was part gnome --
silver braids twirled and tucked

into a comb. She’d send me
to the tavern with a quarter
for a bucket of beer and a nickel
for my strawberry sody.

"She’s baking bread again," said
Old Gregorio in the shack
across the street the morning
he let me ride his old pony.
I pulled a summer’s worth of burrs
from its dusty mane. I felt like Heidi
when he fed me milk and raspberries.

I knew about the coons and rabbits
he shot for food -- the old shotgun
sleeping somewhere behind the kithen door.
He was a poor man after all.
The next summer, shack and pony gone,
Grandma shook her finger, saying,
"Gregorio made a big sin.
Shot his brains out. That’s the one thing
God don’t forgive. Don’t go over there."
I went anyhow, peeked through
the barbed wire of Gregorio’s fence,
and cried for the pony.

MAY-LOUISE, OF TAR RIDGE

When the church kids came
to work on my brother's house,
Harlan took a liking to them.
He talked like I ain't seen him talk
since he lost his arm ten years ago.
The only work he done since then
is growin some cucumbers in the yard.
It ain't that Harlan's no good.
He's just been beaten down these years.
But when he saw them kids tackin screens
and tarrin the roof and buildin steps --
talking to him the whole time --
something in him came back to life.
My God, he started tellin stories.
He told about our brother Johnny
who died a hero in the War,
and about our good mother Thelma.
He even shown them that prize photo
he got of her restin peaceful in her coffin.

And he told them about his "wife" too.
He ain't got no real wife, you see.
He means his shotgun -- "always at his side."
The kids thought he was something all right.
But what got me most was when he put
his wife away and started hammerin nails,
right next to that church boy, Johnny,
who I'm sure was Harlan's favorite.
Johnny says, "What do you call your dogs,
Mr. McQuinn?" and Harlan says,

"I don't call my dogs nothin.
Wouldn't come if I called em anyway."
Well, me and Johnny laughed so hard
we coulda scared a nest of copperheads.

That's the last time I seen Harlan smile
because what them kids don't know is this:
Come September, Harlan started braggin
up his house, and Bates, down the holler,
who still claims our daddy took his land,
said Harlan's braggin about something
ain't even his. Harlan got so mad
he took his wife to Bates' truck,
put eighteen holes in it. Week later?
Harlan's house burned down.
I seen it myself -- just a heap of ashes.
All that's left is them new steps
and some bullets. Harlan's gone,
and I ain't heard from him. Folks say
he's left Rogers, Kentucky,
but I know my brother -- he'll be back.

BETWEEN FRIENDS

Know that I'll soak up your words
like yeast in warm water, but don't

knead me dry. I'm as dependable
as a Rolex but I too demand time.

Use me like a sieve, but no pebbles,
please. Play with me like a child would

but catch the ball if I throw it back.
Fill me like a vase but shatter me

and your feet might bleed. Be as honest
as a tree dropping its leaves gently.

Surprise me but not with distance.
Let me steer when I'm upfront

and I promise that when it's your turn,
I won't be a backseat driver.

Take my gifts but put them in a closet
and Baby, I'm gone.

MADONNA AND CHILD

She wanted a mother
with alabaster arms
and downy hands
to stroke her long, black hair
and speak of Emily Dickinson.

She got a matron,
arms tanned as pie crust,
whose manicured hands
and raspy gin voice
speak of Bloomies
the Club and golf.

But she wanted a daughter,
slim after babies,
jeweled in chains,
chained in plaid,
who would have a house
even bigger than her own.

She got an androgyn,
big and childless,
claid in samurai pants
whose house is nothing
but the world.

RINGS

Tomorrow,
our twentieth anniversary,
and I still can't write
a love poem.
Shall I rub this golden band,
still a bit too big,
but at $5
who could go wrong
at the Frisco Flea Market?
Shazam! It's '71,
and your long, blonde hair,
your riveted jeans,
your black boots
are turning me on.

Now
the jeweler says
they're worth $300 each
and shows me others
that glimmer, their tiny houses
opened like oyster shells,
jewels frilly
as African violets.
But my love,
we've grown so complicated,
who'd trade us in?
If love were a commodity,
we'd be up 295%.
Who could melt us down?

LIGHT UPON THE SAND

When windows fill with icy flora
and the skylight's heaped with fists of snow,
when the wind breaks the willow's branches,

everything begins to creak and shrink,
when the chickadee and cardinal calls
slip through the barren trees

and telephone poles careen like lonely masts,
leave this place awhile.
Return to the gulls and sandpipers,

their twiggy legs a-skitter,
light upon the sand. Leave your footprints.
Taste salt roses. Sit and think.

Watch the waves, your feet encircled
in the foam, and clamshells drying opalescent,
wrapped in seaweed, graceful as calligraphy.

TOWBOAT LULLABY

In the harbor, rocking, rocking,
the towboat sleeps on a lullaby of sea.
Swaying, swaying, she fields the little boats.
Gently, gently, she guides the ocean's waves.
She is wooden and her porous ribs, empty, empty,
parallel the whales. At the mouth of leagues,
she guides the giants. Towing, towing,
she slaps the sea.

I would be that little towboat, resting,
resting, in the harbor's heart. I would pull
the weighty starboards. Easy, Easy,
the waves sift out. For I have learned
the towboat's secret, given, given,
on a leeward night. It's not the ropes
that do the pulling, tautly, tautly,
to the windward sight.

It's not the tension in the towlines, stretching,
stretching, in a spray of salt. It's not
the engine, beating, beating,
that births the vessel out, nor the clever captain
who knows his engine well, steering, steering,
against the frothy swell but the tides themselves
that crest her hull, surely, surely,
as the force that lifts the gulls.

The song from the lips of barnacles,
whispering, whispering,
in the blue salt air, "Don't look back.
The load you pull is there, is there, is there."
Good sailor, remember this: Returning you go
cargoless, lightly, lightly, from the ocean's edge.
Circling, circling, your ropes are drawn
and your dock is fathomless.

HAIKU SEQUENCE

In the reedy marsh
a great blue heron
bill up -- fish down

* * *

Dark calligraphy
of seaweed scattered in sand --
the winter ebbtide

* * *

Great blue heron
gliding gently on the updraft
rising from the marsh

* * *

On the dune trail
sweet sea roses and salt
in the autumn wind

* * *

Clamshells
drying in the sun . . . sandpipers
coming in

* * *

On the hot sand dune --
the everychanging calligraphy
of the wind

* * *

On the hot sand
flickering of a gull's eye --
opalescent clams

BEFORE COMMUNION

Saint Nicholas Cathedral, Ukrainian Village, Chicago

perhaps it is better not knowing the words
only these voices raised a cappella
and this old woman pressing her hands

against the spirit above her
while mosaics spin like Van Gogh's *Starry Night*
and you are surrounded in ova

perhaps it is better not knowing words
only this rail of old faces
who have known too many words

each one a loss
what we all leave behind
until we shape an egg of them

as perfect as this wafer
wild-white and ready
for this sapphire silence

MOSAIC

On a bus from Izmir to Istanbul,
dawn brought a camel caravan
and a hand stroking my face.

I slapped it. Outside, striped riders
rippled the horizon red with shouts.
At the Grand Bazaar, a kind man

served a samovar of tea,
its red leaves richly perfumed
while a gypsy collared a golden bear,

fake jewels dazzling
as it rode a unicyle on command
while he collected.

To shop there is a lust of impulse,
a greed for wares you never wanted
or even knew existed,

and you arrive at your hotel,
arms filled with packages
wrapped in Arabic: a copper plate,

hand-tooled but a little off,
those earrings for the dinner party,
Happy Traveler, who'll find a bauble

missing between the main course
and the dessert. But you won't care.
You've bargained for the strange joy of it.

Inside the *Cathedral Hagai Sophia,*
I stared back
at the Madonna's cracked blue eye,

where time's relentless nail peels
and scratches open golden fragments
lost in plastered walls --

the limp and crumbling finger
of Constantine himself!
Tiny shards of logic revealing

nothing but another mystery.
How strange the sultans' tombs glare
in the courtyard's incongruous sun.

How askew their turbans strain
on sepulchres -- great hornets' nests
impaled on nothing more than sticks.

At the curb, a '57 Chevy,
brightest blue, its driver eager
to please you, take you everywhere,

pretending he won't cheat you
as he leaves you at The Blue Mosque,
where men bow so gracefully

you wish to join them,
where an old woman says
you alone must remove your shoes.

Because poets walk barefoot always,
any exclusion will trouble you,
regardless of your scholarship

which tries, but always fails,
to teach you what to feel.
You must make them disappear

into the muted light,
where no icons interfere
with your frequency to God.

GENUFLECTING

"But when you pray, go away by yourself,
all alone, and shut the door behind you."
. . . MATTHEW 6:6

Faint from lingering incense
and Saint Joseph's languid eye,
I lobbed down on one knee,

surprised that I could floor-burn
on green vinyl masquerading as marble.
In church it was always the same.

But what about those times
when no one watched? I was six.
Mrs. Calahan's served a plate of eggs,

sunny-side up. A dozen slimy eyes,
I thought during Grace,
but they fed us all, her seven and me.

Later, alone in their grease-stained hall,
I crossed myself sideways
beneath their crucifix, poor Jesus --

tarnished, subject to all natural laws.
Maybe it was deference that made me
genuflect. More likely absolution

for wanting to keep my feet clean
while the others romped barefoot
through dust, a clan of tumblers,

shakers, and squealers, these poor
I have always had with me.
At nine, I began genuflecting

from sheer compulsion. Once,
on impulse, I banged my knee
and bowed to a pole that shimmed

up the center of the school's basement.
Perhaps I feared that without
this great, omnipotent pole,

the school could collapse
like a circus tent. Perhaps
I'd fallen into some atavistic

phallic worship. Even then,
I must have been burdened
with a need for private ritual.

I may genuflect to nothing now,
yet a wand of incense curls,
its tail glowing like a comet's

somewhere beyond my skylight.

THE LADY IN BLUE

Solitude is a lady in blue
handing you a gift:

an empty box
wrapped in confusing paper
tied with ticker tape that reads
wrongwaywrongwaywrongway,

the keys to a castle
with forty doors to unlock
one at a time,

an antidote
for the red, bitter berries
you have had to chew,

a pink, neon wand
that burns when you touch it,

a pear seed
that spells healing,
which, when held in your hand
disappears,

a dreamless sleep
stolen in the sunshine
of a January thaw,

a cup of red wine,
aged for forty years,
the clearest and best
you have ever tasted,

a loaf of hot molasses bread
baked for you alone,
eaten with real butter
in big, delicious slices
at your perfect leisure --

a picnic for your soul.

EPIPHANY

-- Moscow, January, 1991

At last the snow that covers the bricks
of Red Square is not tinged with blood,
and the myriad footprints become one
straight line or great circle,
not phantom shadows frozen
in January's white night, massacred
or starved. No longer hungry for flesh,
the bear begins its true journey now,
free to tread the tundra,
play in the snow, wrapped only
in her great, long-awaited spirit.

The people walk to God,
who hid in the swirls of Saint Basil's,
who cried from the souls of the dead,
who lived in Chagall's paintings,
who occupied servant's quarters
in the Hermitage,
who spoke in Nureyev's leaps,
who placed a mark upon the forehead
of the peacemakers,
who waits and works all slow miracles.

Because twenty years ago I walked
in Red Square, stood in long lines
for Lenin's corpse, and oranges,
because I too know the disappointment
of too much thought and theory
and have found church doors locked

in my own country, because I wait
as the eagle dies in the desert,
I need to proclaim this epiphany
with bells. I am burdened,

bundled in a heavy black coat,
a bright, flowered babushka. Never
has the arctic night been so white --
thousands of candles cupped
by hands too used to cold.
The words of the carols are difficult,
buried so long in ice,
thawing now, thawing,
seeping like blood
into the earth which has no choice
but to bear.

KEEPER OF THE HOLY PLACE

If you're lucky, you may find
the church open for confession
or reconciliation. Then enter
like a waif, unattended.
No one will ask you questions.
Commune then with the church itself,
contemplate a single station of the cross,
dwell on the beauty of sapphire glass,
wonder why the archangel cups his hands
around a flame, mandorlas repeating
over archways enclosing you.
Feel the weight of saints,
their staffs bearing down on you,
claim the fear of skulls,
light a candle for no reason,
anonymous, accountable to Whoever
speaks to you in the silence
of a holy place, whose words may be
the silence itself, silence
that makes the sirens bearable.

But because so much else is easy,
America must be hard on pilgrims.
To enter an old cathedral here,
you must call ahead, make arrangements,
get a key, endure a guided tour,
when all you really want

is to be still in a holy place.
In this land of thon-o-thons,
where January is National Blood Month,
where volunteers climb out of closets
to walk, run, swim, and flip
another million pancakes, who will be
the keeper of the holy place?

GIFTS

-- December 23, 1990

You drop in unexpectedly
and bring a perfect gift,
a cut crystal decanter from Czechoslovakia.
Pouring claret into it,
we're charmed as it sparkles
on the white crocheted tablecloth,
the flames of two red candles
caught in its chiseled crevasses.

The fireplace chants softly
from its rounded hearth
as we talk about another year of changes.
You're on the move again,
a woman in the ministry, living
a life so dynamic I tire thinking of it:
relocation, Africa, possibly the Far East.

Twice now you've said,
"You're in a rest period,"
but I tell you it's taken me forty years
to find this peace,
my own still, small voice.
It's taken me more miles
than this poor, old body needs
to find each gift flickering, however bright.

I fill your fluted glass again
and suddenly recall it's Czech too,
a gift from my husband last Christmas.
I give you my latest book of poetry
and wonder if you'll have time to read it,
then see you in a jet stream
nodding when some line hits home.

After you leave early
to meet another group,
my husband and I rub feet in the den,
"Carols from Prague" on A & E.
Placido Domingo is singing "Ave Maria"
in a cathedral warmed only by bodies, breath,
and voices silenced for forty years.

ABOUT THE AUTHOR

Christine Swanberg has written and published poetry for the past ten years, and has had over 100 poems published in over thirty national journals.

An Illinois native and graduate of U. of Wisconsin, she has further degrees from Rockford College and Northern Illinois University as well as post-graduate training from Vermont College.

She has held a number of jobs such as clown, short-order cook, factory worker, nurse's aide, and campaign worker. She has taught English for 15 years.

She currently works as public relations director at Rockford Business College. Founder of Black Earth Poetry Festival, she is an avid reader and presenter as well as consultant and reviewer.

Among her hobbies are travel, horseback riding, making music, and dancing.

She is married and lives in her hometown of Rockford, Illinois.

Grateful acknowledgment is given to the editors of the journals in which most of the poems in SLOW MIRACLE first appeared, sometimes in different form.

Amelia: Oppenheimer, After Forty Years
The Beloit Poetry Journal: Where I Tend My Horse
The Connecticut Writer: Blinded by the Light
Cicada: haiku
Downtown Gazette: Walking Along the Rock River
Dragonfly: haiku
Encore: Shepherdess of Samos
English Journal: An English Teacher's Sonnet
English Journal: For Clara, Third Hour
Farmer's Market: Mushrooms
Farmer's Market: If Dreams Wrote the Story
Frogpond: haiku
Illinois English Bulletin: For Leo Rinaldo
Lucky Star: Dream 167035
Korone: The Day After Christmas
Korone: Lot's Wife's Sonnet
Korone: Moon Sonnet
Korone: Between Friends
Korone: The Light Upon the Sand
Korone: Mosaic
Korone: Genuflecting
Korone: The Lady in Blue
Peninsula Review: At the Bookstore
Peninsula Review: For Dee Greene
Peninsula Review: Coaltown Summers
Life in Atlantis (photo colab.): In the Land of Milk and Honey

Pteranodon: Madonna and Child
Rhino: Tape
Rhino: Dark Night of the Soul
The Rockford Review: In Ephesus
The Rockford Review: A Student Contemplates a Pickled Brain
The Rockford Review: For Keith Jarrett, After a Concert
The Rockford Review: Sonnet After a Performance of Luther
The Rockford Review: Totalled
The Rockford Review: Old Friend
The Rockford Review: Towboat Lullaby
The Rockford Review: May-Louise, of Tar Ridge
The Rockford Review: Rings
The Rockford Review: Camille
Tributary: Before Communion
Tributary: Ice
Tributary: The Butter Guru
Tributary: Burn Out
Willow Review: After watching Vincent and Theo

Swanberg has also been published in The Creative Woman, Great River Review, Kansas Quarterly, Poets On, Sing Heavenly Muse, Mississippi Valley Review, Spoon River Quarterly, Towers, and many others.

OTHER BOOKS BY CHRISTINE SWANBERG:

TONIGHT, ON THIS LATE ROAD (Erie Street Press, 1984)

INVISIBLE STRING (Erie Street Press, 1990)

BREAD UPON THE WATERS (University of Wisconsin: Windfall Prophets Press, 1990)